THE GREAT FIN FRIENDS

To: _________________________

From: _______________________

THE GREAT FIN FRIENDS

Author: Isaiah J. Blakes
Illustrator: Morgan A. Hale

Published by Amber Blakes Consulting, LLC. No part of this publication may be reproduced, distributed, or transmitted in any form or by any means, including photocopying, recording, or other electronic or mechanical methods, without the prior written permission of the publisher, except in the case of brief quotations embodied in critical reviews and specific other noncommercial uses permitted by copyright law.

For permission requests, email the publisher at everythingwithamber@gmail.com. Book Cover Design, Illustrations, and Interior Formatting by Morgan A Hale of Morgan Hale Studios Email: info@morganhalestudios.com

ISBN: 979-8-9904059-2-9 (Print)

This book is dedicated to every reader who needs to know that their differences are what make them special.

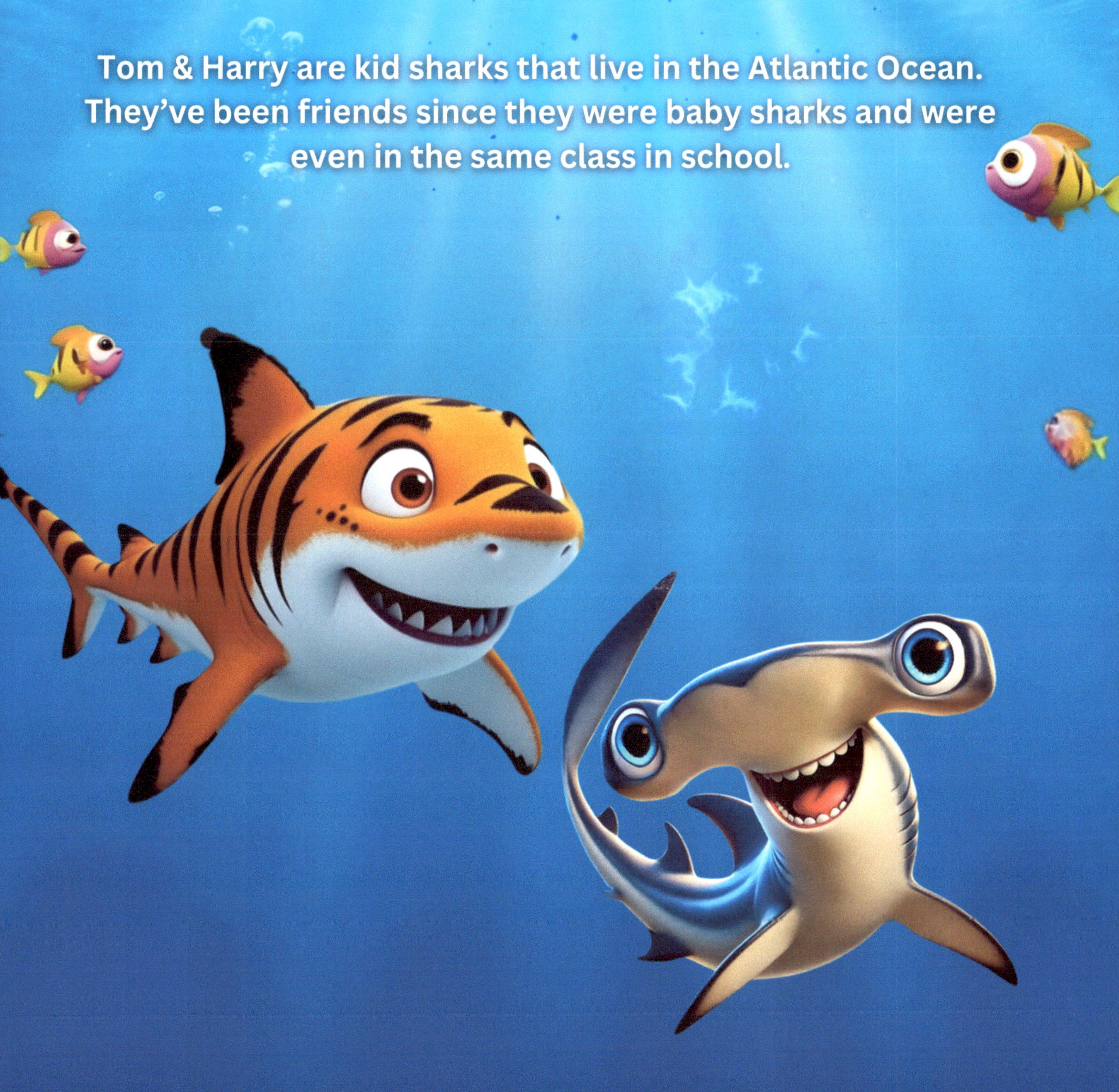

Tom & Harry are kid sharks that live in the Atlantic Ocean. They've been friends since they were baby sharks and were even in the same class in school.

Tom is a big and strong tiger shark with cool black
stripes on his back and sides.

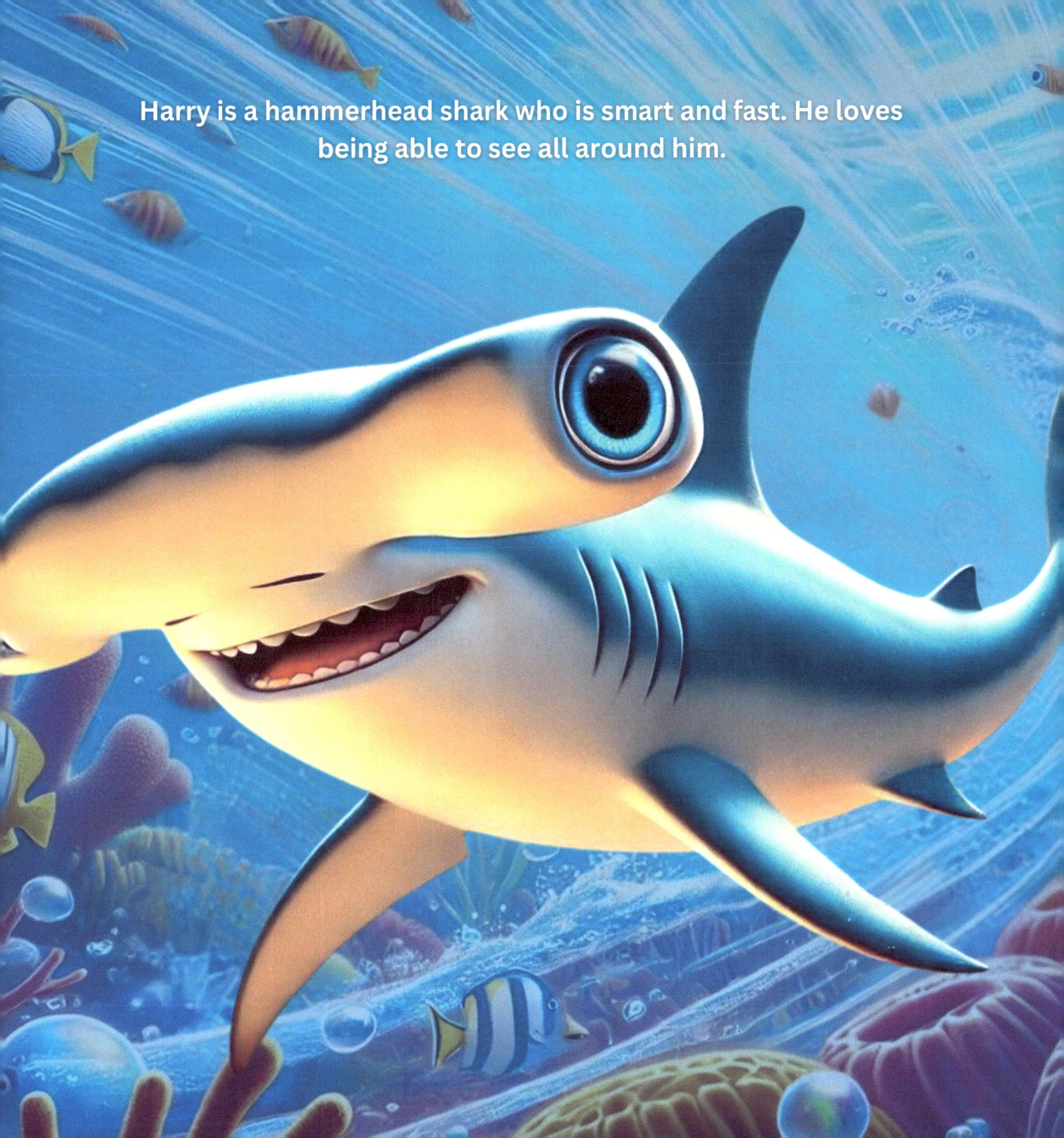
Harry is a hammerhead shark who is smart and fast. He loves being able to see all around him.

They lived with their families in caves next to each other and played together every day.

Their favorite game to play
together was hide and seek.

Their teacher, Mr. Beckham, a bonnethead shark, introduced a new student to the school: Grant, a great white shark.

When it was playtime Grant looked lonely, so Tom and
Harry asked Grant to play hide and seek with them.

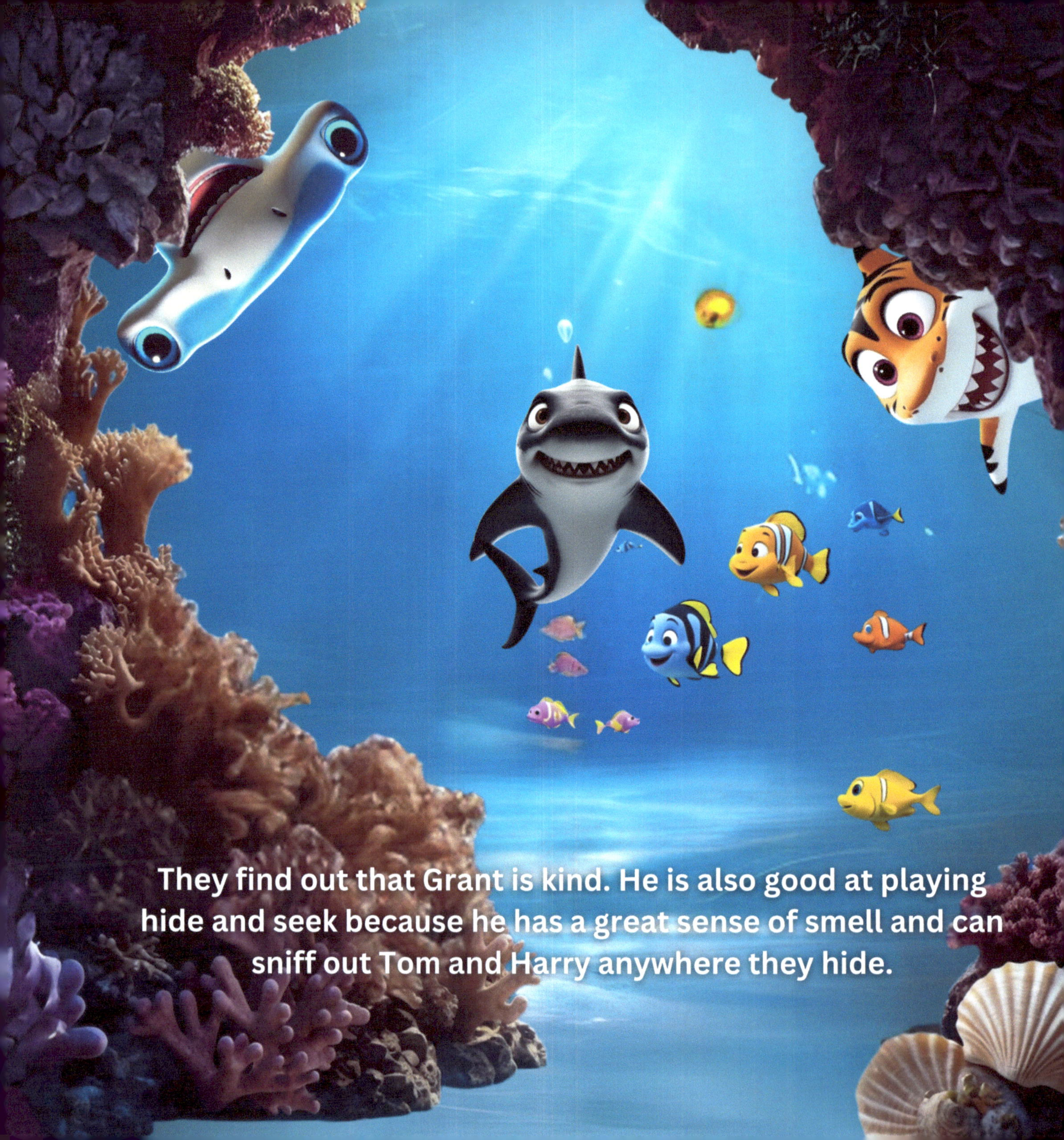

They find out that Grant is kind. He is also good at playing hide and seek because he has a great sense of smell and can sniff out Tom and Harry anywhere they hide.

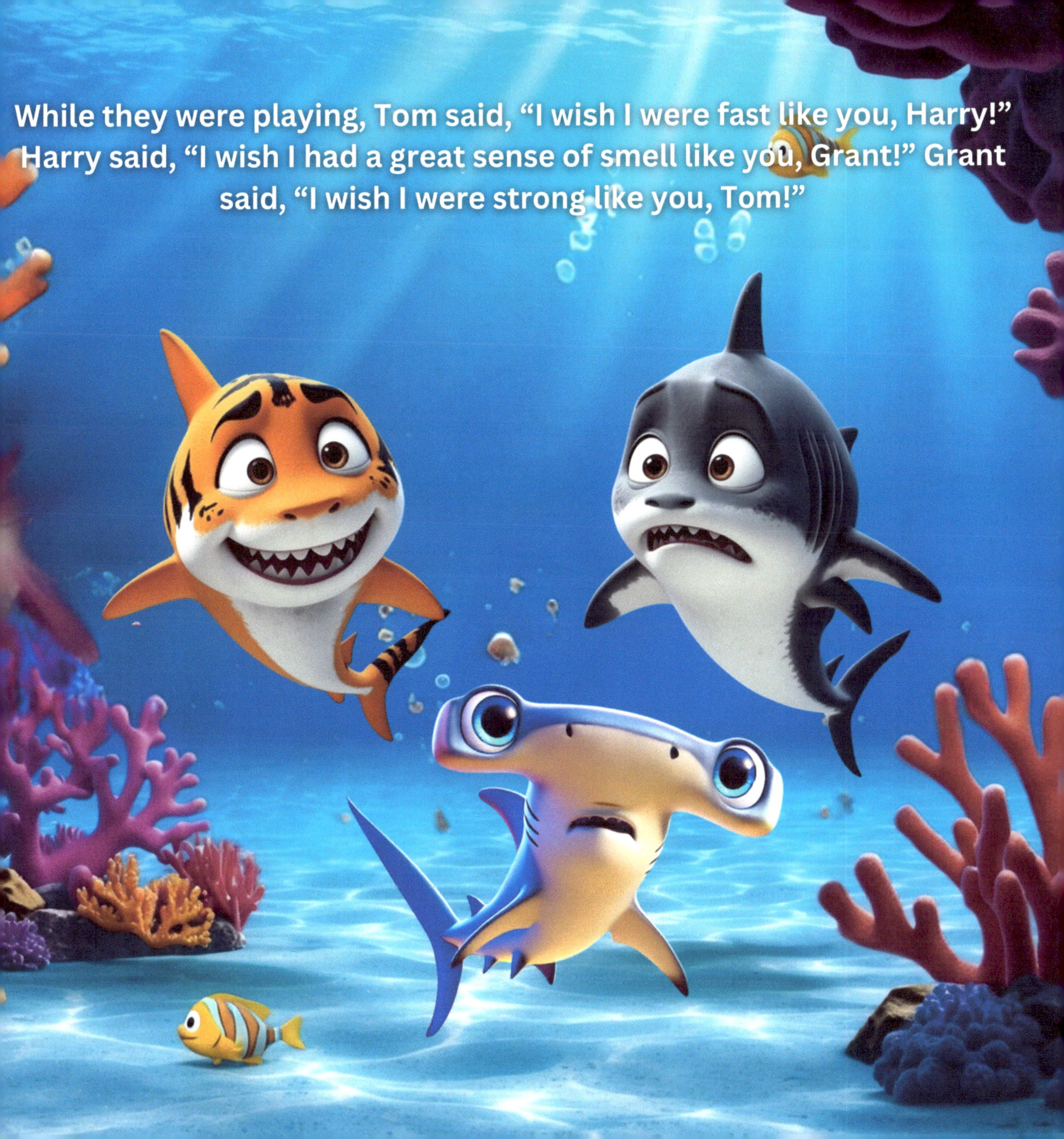
While they were playing, Tom said, "I wish I were fast like you, Harry!" Harry said, "I wish I had a great sense of smell like you, Grant!" Grant said, "I wish I were strong like you, Tom!"

Their teacher, Mr. Beckham, overheard them.

When playtime was over, the three shark friends felt a little sad about not being like each other. Each shark wanted to be special like another friend.

While swimming back to class, Mr. Beckham said to them,
"I heard you three talking earlier."

I want you to know that we are all made differently, and our differences are important. The way you are different makes you special.

Their teacher's words of kindness made Tom, Harry,
and Grant feel better and got them to think.

They began to think about the good parts of themselves and how their differences made each of them special in their own way.

Tom shouted, "We are friends!" Harry shouted, "Great friends!" Grant shouted, "Yeah! Give me some fin!" The three friends happily gave each other a high fin.

Mr. Beckham smiled and said, "Okay, my great fin friends. Let's see how you'll use your differences to help each other from now on."

"For now, let's go back to class and get to work."

THE END!

DID YOU KNOW?

- Tiger sharks are grey with black stripes.

- Hammerhead sharks are fast swimmers.

- Great white sharks have a great sense of smell.

- Bonnet head sharks are also called shovel head sharks.

SHARK WORD SEARCH

Find and circle the words.

W	O	B	G	N	V	G	O	B	L	I	N	Y	M	Q
Z	C	A	R	I	B	B	E	A	N	R	E	E	F	I
J	E	G	E	G	G	B	L	A	C	K	T	I	P	C
C	A	R	A	B	T	D	K	H	R	L	G	B	H	S
O	N	E	T	B	L	U	E	C	T	K	J	A	A	A
O	I	E	W	W	R	W	J	B	U	L	L	S	M	N
K	C	N	H	N	A	F	H	S	M	C	D	K	M	D
I	W	L	I	R	P	I	F	A	P	O	S	I	E	T
E	H	A	T	L	B	O	J	S	L	P	Y	N	R	I
C	I	N	E	T	I	G	E	R	Z	E	N	G	H	G
U	T	D	O	L	Y	P	W	M	Z	G	N	A	E	E
T	E	L	E	M	O	N	M	M	C	F	U	I	A	R
T	T	X	A	L	X	L	U	A	I	W	R	B	D	M
E	I	R	Z	V	R	G	X	F	K	J	S	G	K	U
R	P	T	H	R	E	S	H	E	R	O	E	A	L	H

Great White	Lemon	Thresher	Cookiecutter
Hammerhead	Blue	Blacktip	Greenland
Tiger	Whale	Bull	Carribbean Reef
Oceanic Whitetip	Basking	Nurse	Megamouth
Mako	Goblin	Sand Tiger	Bonnethead

MATCH THE SHARKS

Draw a Line from the shark to its correct name.

A. GREAT WHITE

B. BONNETHEAD

C. HAMMERHEAD

D. TIGER